The Adve

DRY
BONES

By: David C. Atchison
Illustrated By: Marie Weber

Cover design: Marie Weber & David C. Atchison

ISBN 978-0-61520-238-9

Published by Black Bart Books
3447 Little Carpenter Creek Rd.
Fernwood, ID 83830

The Adventures of Black Bart:

DRY BONES

By: David C. Atchison
Illustrated By: Marie Weber

To Kaitlyn, Paul, & Joel
Love, D.A.

To my supportive husband, Bernie and son, Matt, my cat-loving daughter Tanya, and my best friend, Angie. Love, M.

Contents:

Chapter   **Page**

1   Introduction   9

2   Possum   15

3   The Legend   19

4   The Challenge   28

5   Nightmares   34

6   Blinded   41

7   A Bird's Eye View ...   50

8   Dr. Dunnahoo   52

9   A Trap   55

10   Home   62

11   Good News   68

12   Conclusion   74

From the Author   75

Black Bart Sneak Preview   76

Chapter 1

Introduction

 Character is developed by life's experience. Mine is no different. I'm Bart. Some call me Black Bart. I'm the biggest, toughest, meanest house cat that's ever prowled the woods at night. Why, just a low growl from deep in my throat is enough to strike fear in even the ugliest of dogs.

 Humiliation defined my childhood. Dark as midnight with one small patch of white on my chest, they called me "Fuzzball." Fuzzball! Can you believe it! What girl in her right mind would name a great cat like me, "Fuzzball?" Disgusting!

That girl's name was Debbie. Her little brother called her other names. And I was amazed at the names she came up with to call him! She really was quite creative. Come to think of it, she called her brother a lot of names that I would never want to be called. Nevertheless, she had the gall to name me, "Fuzzball!" She couldn't pick "Tom" or "Frank" or "Joe". No, it was "Fuzzball."

People! For some reason no intelligent cat could possibly understand, people are in charge of this planet. In my opinion, cats should rule. After all, cats are smarter, more athletic, better at taking care of themselves, and most are far better looking. Cats always know what they want. I've watched people become rather annoyed with us at times when we ask to go in the house and then turn around and ask to go out. They're not even smart enough to realize we are training them to do our bidding.

People rarely seem to care about the important things in life. Things like how to make a cat's life more comfortable, more interesting, and more exciting. For example, many people love to have cats in their house, but they rarely bring other animals like chipmunks, squirrels, and birds in the house for a cat to chase. Instead they buy little toys. Or worse…dogs! This forces us to prowl around elsewhere to look for most of our entertainment.

People are generally thoughtless, selfish, and completely egotistical. Without a good cat to help them, purr on their lap, and listen to them ramble, most are completely lost. Cats provide purpose in a person's life. As far as I'm concerned, cats do so much for their people that a person's sole reason for living should be to make a cat's life more comfortable. Yet, with that said, some people can't even come up with a decent name for a self-respecting cat. Fuzzball! The memory would bring tears to my eyes. If cats cried, that is. Cats don't cry, they yowl! After all, if a cat is suffering, someone else is going to suffer with it. Fuzzball!

What's in a name anyway? Some of the toughest cats I know started out life as "Little One", "Sissy", "Puss-n-boots", and "Snowball". Why even John Wayne, one of the best known tough guys of the twentieth century, started out life with the name Marion. Like I said, experience develops character.

Just the same, people have their place, and with time and patience they can be trained to do just about anything. When they cater to cats, they do more than keep the cat dish full. People are great at opening doors, providing furniture on which to sleep and sharpen claws, picking up old cat hair with their clothes, and, well, you get the point. Why, they'll even keep a cat box clean!

Some people are easily distracted and get confused about what is really important in life, and with their size and everything, they can be a little unmanageable. That's where patience comes in. Just keep in mind that they aren't as intelligent as cats, and give them a little room. Some people say cats think they are people themselves, just smaller. Yeah right! Did I mention that people can be arrogant, too? They often think they are better than cats. Can you believe that? They seem to forget that if they weren't so big, we would chase them down, corner them, and eat them. But, that's enough about people. This story is about me.

Not only did I start out in life with a lousy name, but I was a runt. And if that wasn't enough, I lost my mother before I was weaned. I resorted to drinking milk from a baby bottle just to survive. Nothing works better than warm milk from a bottle to fatten up a kitten. It tasted so good!

When I couldn't get my mouth around a milk bottle I would settle for sucking on Debbie's little finger. The finger sucking thing is a disgraceful habit that I still haven't kicked. My advice to you is, "Don't start!" Trying to quit sucking fingers is like trying to quit taking naps. Just when you think you've got it conquered, WAMO! You find yourself purring on some person's lap, sucking their little finger, and falling asleep. It might feel good at the time, but the humiliation lasts forever.

Now, before you go judging me for my name and the fact that I was a runt who had to drink from a baby bottle, just remember a certain member of the swine family named "Wilbur". How would you like that name? Wilbur! Why, that has to be worse than Fuzzball. And "pig". They always referred to him as a pig. Now while it's technically true, it is somewhat demeaning. Not once have I heard him called a hog or a boar! That's kind of like calling a cat a kitty-kitty or a pussycat!

If you'll think back, you'll also remember that Wilbur was a runt, and was fed milk from a baby bottle just like me. Yet, with the help of a talented spider, he became a very well known swine. Oh, by the way, I bet you didn't know that if someone got a few fingers too close to Wilbur's snout, he would suddenly latch on, start sucking, and quietly grunt himself to sleep. Humiliation!

Have you ever noticed that only people can be veterinarians? It is a person's only chance of keeping cats from taking over the world. House cats are almost completely self reliant, but if we get sick or injured we're at the mercy of people. To think a cat is at the mercy of anyone is, in itself, a humbling experience. A lot of cats just give up trying to be respectable, settle down on a soft couch, and eat and sleep their way into obese oblivion.

Obesity! I was the fattest kitten you ever saw. It wasn't being fat that bothered me so much; it was just that other kittens could be so mean! They wouldn't leave me alone. They'd call me things like Tubby, Pudgy, Fatty, and Lardball. It was all very humiliating. The only way I could ever gain respect after that was to get in shape and become a hunter. In my neighborhood, hunters were looked up to and highly regarded.

I was sick of being pushed around. I decided I would turn my fat into muscle and earn some respect. No longer would I be called Fuzzball. From now on my name would be Bart, Black Bart to some. Even the people in my life would soon admit that I'd outgrown the name Fuzzball.

It was autumn, and the days were often very cool. The leaves on the apple tree in our front yard were starting to turn yellow and fall off, providing a little entertainment as I chased them across the yard when the wind blew. That soon got boring, and I started taking regular long walks in the crisp night air for exercise.

My favorite place to roam was the woods behind our house. Sometimes I was gone for days. I was walking, playing in the bushes, running after my shadow, stretching and scratching on trees, and doing all sorts of activities I thought would help build muscle. It worked great! By mid-winter, I had turned my entire thirty pounds into solid muscle.

All the other cats thought I was out hunting, but really I was getting into shape. I don't know what they thought I was hunting. There seemed to be very few animals in the woods, just the occasional bird chirping high in the dark pine trees above me, or a lone chipmunk or squirrel chattering now and then. Fortunately, that didn't seem to matter. In their mind I was hunting, I was successful, and I was a mystery. Why else would I keep going back to the woods so regularly? Their perception was not a problem. I was happy to be considered the biggest, toughest, meanest house cat that's ever prowled the woods at night.

Chapter 2

Possum

Once a cat earns a good reputation, he has to keep it up. I had long since trained the people in my life to open doors, give me milk on demand, and stay off my favorite chair. They respected me. Cats, however, aren't as easy to impress. While the other cats didn't dare challenge me physically, they kept watching for a weakness. They respected me because of my size, and they were sure I knew how to use it. They watched me turn from a fat cat into a muscle machine in just a few months.

Most cats are known to kill mice and birds around the house. If they are especially good hunters, you might see them catch an occasional squirrel or rabbit and lay it by the door to their house. It's funny. Some people see an animal left at the door by a cat and think, "Gross!" Other, slightly more intelligent people are impressed, but think to themselves, "Hey, the cat is bringing us some food. The poor thing doesn't realize we don't eat animals that cats bring us."

This just shows how little people really know. Cats don't bring their catch to the door to share food with people. Cats don't like sharing, and in my opinion, they shouldn't have to! We like showing off and teaching others not to mess with us because we're born killers. In fact, cats are the greatest hunters on earth. We know people won't eat what we bring them. That's why we do it. Our catch must stay by the door long enough for the other cats to see it, so they know how good we are. Respect from your fellow cat is a reward greater than fresh meat any day of the week. It's the equivalent of trophy hunting.

The weather was mild with no snow on the ground. I was walking through the woods, getting my morning exercise and minding my own business, when a gray squirrel tried to run in front of me. Notice I said, "tried." Instinct took over. With a swipe of one paw I scooped him up and flung him against a nearby rock. I pounced, landing directly on top of him, expecting him to struggle so I could make the kill. Then, just when I was about to go for the jugular, I realized he wasn't moving. By hitting him against the rock, I must have knocked him out cold. At this point, some cats would have killed him anyway, quickly eaten part of him, and then brought the rest to the door to show off. Most are better sports than that. We enjoy a challenge.

I felt I was the best of good sports. Having lived through unfortunate humiliation as a kitten, I knew how horrible it was to be kicked when you're down. I wanted this squirrel to think he had a fighting chance. I wanted him to die knowing he fought hard and died with honor. I wanted the other squirrels watching from the trees to see their pal fight a brave battle with a huge tom cat. Instead, they would see their unsuspecting friend die from a lucky swipe by an overgrown house cat.

I licked his face. He woke up to what must have been a horrifying situation. There he was, pinned tight to the ground by my razor sharp claws and staring into my hungry eyes. My plan was to let him go with all but one front paw; make him feel like he was doing well, like he had a chance before I pinned him down again. I would repeat the process several times; each time giving him the hope, and the slight chance, for escape. You may have seen cats do this with mice. People think we are torturing and playing with them. The truth is that cats are normally such good hunters that unless we give them several chances to escape, we can't really take pride in our success. Pride is what a cat lives for.

Now, this squirrel was a bit twisted in the mind. Instead of showing fear and panicking to get away, he blinked a few times, smiled, and introduced himself. "Hi, I'm Possum," he said. "It is very kind of you to spare my life. What can I do for you in return?"

I wanted to scream, "Run! Fight! Bite! Claw! Do anything but just lay there!" Instead, I found myself being polite. It seems that a quiet word turns away wrath. My ferocious intensity turned into curiosity. My intention to kill was reduced to polite, well almost polite, conversation. "My name is Bart, Black Bart to some. I'm the biggest, toughest, meanest house cat that's ever prowled the woods at night."

"Of course you are," Possum replied. "That's why you would never need anything from me. Still, I have an idea that might interest you. It's an idea you might benefit from."

"You mean besides tearing you apart and dragging the leftovers back to the doorstep?" I have to admit, this was one brave squirrel, or else just plain stupid.

Chapter 3

"The Legend"

"**E**very animal knows cats are proud hunters. They love to show off and bring impressive trophies back to the doorstep of their house. What's the biggest trophy you've ever seen a cat bring home?" Possum inquired.

I thought back to a legendary hunter I'd known in my youth. His name was Tiki. While he was only about half my size, he was strong and quick. I once watched him corner a mouse, frighten it so much that all it could do was stand there and shake, then walk away to show the other cats that a mouse was too small and bony to be worth the effort. Tiki went wherever he wanted, he did whatever he wanted, and he slept anywhere he pleased day or night.

"It was a rabbit," I replied. "It was at least four times your size." I emphasized this point just in case Possum was starting to feel safe. I was beginning to get the idea that no matter what happened, I wouldn't be able to kill this friendly squirrel. But Possum didn't need to know that.

The conversation brought back old memories. I'm sure my eyes must have glazed over as I thought about the great cat I had looked up to as a kitten. I could remember it like it was yesterday.

It was a hot summer afternoon when Tiki brought that rabbit up the stairs to his house. It was still kicking its back legs, helplessly trying to get away. Tiki then proceeded to eat it alive, head first, in front of all of us. A lasting impression was made, and Tiki's reputation was sealed. Tiki was hard to figure out, yet one thing was certain. Tiki was the best hunter any of the neighborhood house cats had ever seen.

That was Tiki's trick. Bring his prey back alive and either let it go, or eat it in front of all the other cats. Come to think of it, I never saw Tiki eat another animal after that rabbit. Why, even in his old age, he would regularly bring back live squirrels and let them go, just so he could taunt the younger hunters. Yet, he was the only house cat able to hunt successfully in the woods. He'd hunted the woods so well that the other cats quit even looking for wild game there. It seemed that Tiki had hunted the game nearly to extinction, or scared it off to parts unknown.

I may have been the biggest, toughest, meanest house cat ever to prowl the woods at night, but Tiki held the title as the greatest hunter of all time. He was a true legend. He seemed to be in the right place at the right time to catch animals that we would never even see. What I wouldn't give to have Tiki's reputation.

Now don't tell anyone, but the truth is that Possum was the first animal I'd ever caught. You see, I was taken from my mother before she had the chance to teach me how to hunt. All I'd really ever done was chase a furry ball full of catnip around the house. I would often pretend it was a nasty little mouse. I would bite it, bat it, chase it down, pounce on it, and bite it again. I experienced all the fun of hunting a mouse without having to touch the real thing.

I was afraid of mice. Not because I was a chicken, a wimp, or a scaredy cat. No, it was more like the way a cat is afraid of water. Sure a house cat can jump into water and swim. But why would it want to? It isn't like we don't keep ourselves clean.

Mice give me the creeps, with their boney little bodies and beady little eyes. I've heard they taste quite good, but I can't imagine eating one. They're just bones and fur as far as I can tell. Catnip is much better. So, I left the mice to the other cats.

At first this helped build my reputation among them. I'd just leave without telling anyone where I was going or what I was doing. The other neighborhood house cats would watch me silently wander through the fence and past the alley into the woods. They all figured I was above hunting mice and went to the woods in search of bigger prey. They knew how hard it was to find something to hunt in Tiki's old hunting ground, so the fact that I kept going back led them to believe I was successful. I never brought anything back with me, but that was easily explained. The other cats just figured I ate my catch for survival. Their imaginations were completely on my side. I loved my walks, but it was hunger that always brought me back home. Nothing beats a nice bowl of milk.

Well, back to Possum. He started to tell me all about this deal he had once made with another cat. It turned out that this old hunter's name was Tiki. "Tiki was a great hunter," Possum said, "but he was getting old and had to start on a special prescription food that his people bought from the local veterinarian. He knew he couldn't keep eating wild game for long and was having problems keeping up with the younger cats; I can only assume he meant you. So, Tiki came up with a plan."

"Tiki decided that in order to protect his reputation, he was going to have to be ruthless. From that point on, every animal he caught would be given a choice. It could either agree to trust him and talk its friends and family into meeting with him, or it could run, be caught, and suffer the consequences. Then, he would let it go. If it chose to run, he would chase it down, drag it to the house alive, and eat it in front of the other cats. That's what happened to the biggest wild rabbit in the woods. We called him 'Hopper'. I'm sure he's the same one you saw being eaten on the doorstep. I was there, sitting quietly in a branch above them, when he was caught the second time."

Possum continued, "I overheard Tiki explaining to Hopper that if he hadn't run, if he had trusted him, he would have lived. He apologized for what he had to do next and explained to the terrified rabbit that if nothing else, he had to be a cat of his word. He said Hopper would suffer the consequences if he ran, and that is exactly what he meant."

"It broke my heart to see Hopper pleading for his life as he was drug back to the house. Hopper had made his decision. It was too late to change his mind now. I couldn't watch what happened next and was overcome by a terrible fear."

"What did you do?" I asked, completely wrapped up in Possum's story and forgetting that I had planned to do nearly the same thing to him.

"Let me tell you," Possum said, "for a squirrel, fear is like a flea bite. It always gets your attention. The name of the flea is either Common Sense or Panic. It's the squirrel's job to figure out which one is doing the biting. More times than not, it's Common Sense. Panic usually gets you into a heap of trouble."

"I thought about the choice Tiki gave Hopper. I know why Hopper did what he did. He thought running away from what scared him was his best chance to survive, while bringing his friends and family out to meet Tiki was a trap that would endanger them all. He hoped that by escaping, ignoring, and avoiding Tiki, he could just enjoy life. Denying that there are consequences to our choices never protects us from the aftermath. Now tell me, Bart, you're a big strong cat and probably a mighty hunter. How many rabbits can a cat catch at one time?"

I thought for a moment, "Only one." I knew that all the other rabbits would be long gone by the time one was caught.

"That's right! So if Tiki had already caught Hopper, why would he give him a choice? It wasn't because he thought he could catch more that one rabbit at a time. No, cats are too smart for that. Hopper, after all, was the largest rabbit in the woods. If Tiki really meant harm, he wouldn't have bothered telling Hopper anything. It must have been for another reason. I just had to find out.

So the next day, I scurried down from my tree perch right in front of Tiki. In an instant I was pinned to the ground by his sharp claws. I kept my cool. I knew from watching cats hunt that if things got bad, I could pretend to be dead. Most house cats get their food from people and are proud hunters that want their prey to fight back. I figured that if I lay perfectly still, like I was already dead, a house cat would set me down and walk proudly around in a circle, giving me a chance to catch it off guard and escape to a tree. I've done it before. That's how I got my name, Possum."

I laughed so hard I started to choke and coughed up a large slimy hair ball onto Possum's chest. When I was finally able to talk again I exclaimed, "You mean to tell me that you let Tiki catch you! You must be several nuts short of a cache, because that's just insane! They should have started calling you, 'Nuts!'"

Possum shook like a dog after a bath and some of my own saliva splattered back into my face. "It wasn't as crazy as you might think. In fact, it probably saved my life. So there I was, wondering if that was the end, when Tiki whispered into my ear the same two choices he'd given Hopper the night before. When he let me go, I just stood there. I told him I would try to get my friends and relatives to meet with him, but couldn't promise they would come. He walked away saying, 'Good enough. I'll see you tomorrow, then.'"

"Did they come?" I asked.

"Of course they didn't come! Do you think squirrels are crazy?" Possum replied indignantly.

"So what did you do?" I questioned, not sure what he would say this time.

"I came back," he snickered. "Tiki was bound to catch me again if I didn't."

"I rest my case!" I said, shaking my head. "Maybe your friends and relatives aren't nuts, but I have no doubt that you are."

Possum continued to explain to me that instead of Tiki dragging him to the doorstep and eating him in front of the others, they acted in a way that would ultimately impress the other cats without doing any harm to Possum.

Tiki and Possum did it again and again. Sometimes Possum's friends would take a turn. Even when Tiki got so old he could hardly leave the house, he would nonchalantly walk around a tree, and amazingly, come waltzing back to the door with another squirrel in his mouth. He'd glare at the other cats, swish his tail back and forth, and then let the squirrel go.

I was one of those watching. To us, Tiki's hunting finesse was incredible. We never realized it was Possum who had been brought back almost every time. It's a good thing, too! I was humiliated enough as a kitten. I don't know how I would have taken the news that I could be fooled so easily. However, the thought that I might be able to fool the other neighborhood house cats brought a smile to my face.

None of us had dared chase an animal Tiki had just let go, lest he drag us to the doorstep. Cats don't like to share. If any cat interfered with another cat's display of hunting prowess, it would mean a fight and certain disgrace. If the interfering cat lost the fight, it would be shamed by loosing. If it won, it would be disgraced by stealing prey from the weaker cat rather than getting its own. It was best to simply respect the other hunters.

It turns out that Tiki and Possum became great friends. Tiki taught many of the woodland creatures how to stay away from house cats. This left the others nothing but filthy little mice and the occasional bird to catch. And Possum, in return, provided companionship to his new friend. As long as no new predators moved into the woods, the woodland creatures would be safe.

Possum mourned his friend with deep sorrow when Tiki passed away. He missed the tag games, and never forgot the way Tiki would pin Possum to the ground while carefully keeping his sharp claws tucked inside his velvety paws. When others thought Tiki was biting Possum, he was usually telling him one of his bad mouse jokes. It was all Possum could do not to laugh as Tiki stared down the other cats and let him go.

Chapter 4

A Challenge

Things had changed since Tiki's reign. And, once again, ignorance on someone else's part, as well as their vivid imaginations, gave me an advantage. You see, it became so rare for a cat to hunt in the woods that some of the woodland creatures began to leave the safety of the trees and run and play on the forest ground, while just a few squirrels kept a lookout in the trees. The animals knew it was time to seek a hiding place when a squirrel started to chatter, so the house cats had no idea there were more than just a few squirrels and birds hiding safely in the trees. The woods were really as full as ever with a variety of life.

Then it happened. A cat came back. Only this time it was the biggest housecat they had ever seen. At first I seemed to them quite overweight, but they also noticed that I kept coming back. Each time I looked a little bit stronger, and a little bit meaner. They soon realized that I was the biggest, toughest, meanest house cat ever to prowl the woods at night. Of course, it was just me getting my exercise. They thought I was hunting.

Most of the animals hid as usual, using the tricks Tiki had showed them for avoiding the attention of other house cats. While they hid, Possum watched. It wasn't long before he noticed I wasn't slow, wasn't quiet, and certainly wasn't sneaking around trying to surprise some poor creature. In Possum's mind, I was so bold, so proud, and so good that I didn't have to sneak around like other house cats. Possum decided I must be more deadly than any of them. He decided I must be even more dangerous than Tiki was in his youth. He thought that every time I took a walk in the woods I was studying trails, marks, patterns, smells, and noises.

He was right, but not for the reason he supposed. I loved it in the woods. It wasn't always quiet, but it was always peaceful. When the birds, chipmunks, and squirrels yelled to each other, warning of my presence, it was like a sweet melody drifting to my ears on the otherwise quiet breeze.

Possum, however, decided that I was just gathering information so I could start picking them off one at a time. Once again he was overcome by a terrible fear. And, once again, Possum decided to put himself in harm's way in order to save his friends and relatives. Only this time, he was wrong. I had never given a choice of freedom or safety to any animal. Actually, I was looking forward to my first real kill. How could he know that I wouldn't just kill and eat him? However, the only creatures I really threatened were those stupid enough to run right in front of me. Stupid.....or crazy! But the information I gave to Possum was on a need to know basis only. He didn't need to know that I couldn't hunt.

After all, I wanted to be known as an even greater hunter than Tiki. Tiki was a legend. And like most legends, this one kept growing long after Tiki was gone. Story after story would grow out of proportion until Tiki's life became a tall tale that all the other house cats believed as true. There were stories about Tiki successfully fighting off bobcats and hawks, owls and coyotes, even a badger or two. How dogs would tuck their tails and slowly back away anytime Tiki came near. They even told of the scars on old Brandy's face. Brandy was a cat-killing guard dog who hated anything that moved. Few cats entered Brandy's yard and lived to tell about it. Most who said they did were lying.

I decided to walk Brandy's fence once as part of my training. After all, what good is strength without balance and agility? The other cats watched me, expecting yet another cat to either jump off the fence and run in fear, or die bravely. I knew I could do it. After all, I was Bart! I was also wrong.

The first time Brandy growled and jumped against the fence, I lost my balance. Instead of

letting the other cats see me fall, I jumped. Fortunately, I landed on my feet and ran straight into
the only hiding place I could find. It also happened
to be Brandy's dog house.

He was after me at lightning speed. Enough
drool to drown most cats went spraying everywhere as his jowls slapped in all directions like a
kite flapping in a strong wind. There was no time
for my life to flash before my eyes. I had to do
something. Fortunately, there was a hole in the
back of the dog house big enough for me to get
through, but not big enough for Brandy. I escaped
just in time and jumped to the top of the dog house
to stay away from his snapping jaws.

Brandy, being a stupid dog, tried to go head
first through the hole in the back of his dog house
and got his collar stuck on the rough boards.
When the other cats heard Brandy stop growling
and start whining like a puppy being taught a lesson
by a few sharp claws to the nose, they jumped on
the fence to see what happened. All they saw was
me standing on the dog house and Brandy's big
back end sticking out of the front with his stubby
little tail tucked between his legs while he continued to whimper pitifully.

I walked proudly back to the wooden fence,
used my claws to help me get to the top, jumped
down, and walked away without a word. Brandy
didn't bother me again for quite some time. When I
jumped on the fence after that, he would immediately head for his dog house, being careful not to

stick his head in the hole in the back wall. I had no idea whether or not his face had any scars.

I explained to Possum that I didn't need his help building a reputation. I already had one, and it was good. I knew I couldn't compete with Tiki's hunting prowess just by bringing back a squirrel and letting it go. If Possum wanted to stay alive and help me earn the reputation as the greatest hunter of all time, he would have to do better than that. Otherwise, I would simply start picking off his friends and family one at a time. So Possum asked if I would give him a night to think, and if I would keep from hunting any woodland creatures until then.

"Sure," I replied. "I'll see you tomorrow, then." I was feeling quite happy with myself as I trotted along the trail that led out of the woods. I was sure that Possum would come up with a superb plan. I reached the fence, squeezed through the loose boards, and strutted into my back yard.

I was greeted by what seemed to be a curious mob of other house cats. They knew better than to demand anything from me, but they wanted to know why, out of all the times I went hunting in the woods, I had never brought anything back to show them. Some said they wanted to see one of my awesome trophies but would be happy if I just brought back a few leftover mouse bones. Others suggested that I wasn't hunting at all and probably didn't know how, since I was raised on a milk bottle.

Can you believe it? Nobody, and I mean **NOBODY**, was going to humiliate me again! So how did I reply? Deep down in my throat I let out a low growl and then proceeded to stride through the mob with my head held high in silence. They stepped aside as if making way for a king. They knew I meant business. And I knew that my reputation had been challenged.

I went straight to the house, sharpened my claws on the heavy wooden front door until my girl let me in, and then yowled at the refrigerator door until it produced a nice bowl of milk. What a day I had! I was exhausted!

After finishing my bowl of milk, I went looking for a soft warm place to sleep. So far today I'd gone to the woods to get some exercise, caught my first animal, made friends with it, and let it go! I started to think that maybe I was the nutty one. I jumped up onto my girl's lap, started purring as I sucked on her little finger, and fell fast asleep.

Chapter 5

Nightmares

I woke up alone on the couch just before nine o'clock that night. Debbie had been careful not to wake me as she moved to get ready for bed. I slept soundly for a while, yet my dreams were very disturbing. I had become in my dreams the great hunter I always wanted to be. Unfortunately, it was a terrible experience. I dreamt of catching different animals over and over again. I drug each one back alive to the door and ate them in front of all the other cats. Their cries for mercy blended together into a symphony that for me meant total agony. Nightmares!

Utterly haunted, I was unable to fall back to sleep. The dreams had even ruined my appetite. The pleas that came from my prey were still echoing in my head. I had to find some measure of peace. But how could I do that? The only thing I could think of was to seek out Possum and ask for his forgiveness. I allowed him to believe I was the kind of cat that would hunt down his family one at a time and eat them alive in front of the other hunters. I knew that wasn't me.

I yowled at the door. Great! My girl woke up immediately and let me outside. I had no idea where I might find Possum at this time of night.

He might even be sleeping, for all I knew. I snuck silently around the back of the house to the edge of the lawn and slid between the two loose boards in the wooden fence that ran the length of the alley behind the houses on our block. I didn't want to alert the other cats of my expedition for fear they might expect me to bring something back.

The small forest was one quarter mile wide and one quarter mile deep and started just beyond the alley past the back yard fence. There were 40 acres of trees at all stages of growth. Finding a squirrel in that area would be quite a challenge. I started to head toward the same tree where I had last seen Possum.

When I reached the tree I thought about yowling to let Possum know I was there, and then changed my mind. If he was asleep, he would be too well hidden to find anyway, and I could wait until morning. I hated being disturbed during a nap, so I reasoned that Possum would, too. If he was awake, he would be watching for me. I decided to keep walking and see if he found me.

The woods were particularly quiet. The moon was full and cast long shadows everywhere. I was well camouflaged in the midst of the darkest shadows, but I should have been easily seen when the moonlight reflected off my shiny black fur. I walked for hours, surprised that the squirrels hadn't signaled their usual warning. The silence was anything but peaceful.

If you've ever walked in the woods, you know it's easy to get lost. What would be a comfortable walk in a field becomes a nearly impossible maze of trees. I had spent so much time in these woods that I had learned the intricate pathways that weaved themselves throughout the entire 40 acres. I never did find Possum that night, and the only sound I heard sent chills down my spine. It wasn't the lonely howl of a wolf, the eerie cry of coyotes, or the shrill scream of a hawk. It was a catlike "MEEE-Owww"; the voice of another predator in the woods on that moonlit night making it clear that no other hunters would be tolerated.

The sound was followed by a low, "Whoo-hoo hoooooo hoo." I knew that it was a Great Horned Owl, an enormous bird with very large yellow-orange eyes and a small brain. Despite their obvious inferiority to cats, these owls are fantastic hunters. They are so good that some people call them Cat Owls or Winged Tigers, not to mention their uncanny ability to sound like a cat. Their wingspan can reach up to five feet. Huge sharp talons allow them to instantly kill most of their prey as they swoop down in silence. I had never known of a Great Horned Owl nesting in this particular woods before, yet realized exactly what it meant. Few animals would be safe from this new predator. These owls have been known to swallow rodents and small rabbits whole. Anything bigger would be ripped apart by their powerful beaks and swallowed in chunks.

Obviously, I was too big for the owl to try to eat whole, but I didn't care to tangle with it in any case. I listened carefully, trying to determine where the sound was coming from. I now knew why the other animals were so quiet and decided to give up trying to find Possum. I stayed silent and walked close to the trees, hidden by the shadows as I continued to listen for the owl's location.

Just then, I stepped on something large and round. I jumped back, and then pounced on it. It seemed to be a hard hairball of some kind. I bit into it. It tasted nasty. It was hard and dry, but broke when I bit into it. It was an owl pellet. Owls often swallow their prey whole, and then cough up what cannot be digested. Inside the hard brown pellet were bones, dry bones. Ah-ha! This was just the evidence I needed to prove my hunting prowess. The other cats would no longer doubt that I was indeed hunting in the woods. As I thought about my deception, I forgot all about my noble plan to come clean. My reputation would be safe, for now.

I put the pellet into my mouth and, more quietly then I'd ever been before, headed home. It was well past midnight when I got to the back fence. I was glad to see that the boards were still loose, because it was by far the easiest way into the yard. My people must have known I used that hole regularly to go to the woods, and I'm sure they left the boards loose for my convenience.

I no longer cared to keep my activities a secret. In fact, I couldn't wait to cough up a bone-filled hairball right in front of the other cats. I set the pellet down in the tall grass and let out a mighty growl, followed by a triumphant "Yeeeeee-Oooowwwll!"

I could hear the cats coming from all over the neighborhood. I quickly put the pellet back in my mouth. When the first of the cats arrived, I glared at them while I swished my tail back and forth. Then, I started to cough. It was difficult to keep the broken pellet in my cheeks as I coughed so long and so hard that I expelled every last bit of air from my lungs. I did it again and again, waiting for my audience to get close enough to see me produce the horrid ball of hair and slime. By keeping it in my mouth, the pellet became much softer and the small bones poked into my cheeks. I spit it out right in front of the others, lifted my head high, and strutted home without another word.

From my perspective, the night that started out with haunting dreams had ended in total success. Had I experienced that night from Possum's point of view, however, I would have thought quite differently.

It was just after eight in the evening when Possum heard the first great "MEEE-Owww!" coming from the trees. He had never before heard such a cry and didn't dare start chattering to warn the others. First, there was no doubt it was heard by all the other creatures. Second, Possum could not tell where it was coming from and didn't want to make himself a target for some new cat's trophy. Fear was becoming an all too normal feeling for Possum.

As quietly as possible, Possum began to search for what he thought was a cat he'd heard. It is said curiosity killed the cat. Possum wondered if it would kill the squirrel. Then he saw me. Only this time I wasn't strutting confidently, or friskily bounding through the forest. I was sneaking, or so it appeared to Possum. Possum was confident that the eerie meow he'd heard earlier was me. He'd never heard me yowl, and didn't know what to expect. That the sound had come from an owl didn't even cross his mind.

He followed me for a while, watching as I walked in and out of the dark shadows. I looked unsettled and my tail twitched. Was I hunting this time? He wasn't sure. He really didn't want to find out if I was. Then he heard a loud, "Whoo-hoo hoooooo hoo."

It was then that Possum decided I must be hunting that owl. He decided that maybe I didn't need his help to build and keep a great reputation after all. A cat that can catch an owl is a great hunter indeed. He was concerned that, if this was true, he and his friends and relatives might be in graver danger than he thought. At this, Possum stopped following me and waited for my return. He almost expected me to bring an owl back in my mouth. As it turned out, that is not what he saw at all.

Possum happened to be watching from high in a tree near the pellet I'd found on the ground. He didn't hear me coming. He didn't see me walking stealthily among the dark shadows. Then suddenly he saw something pounce. It was me. He couldn't tell what I had pounced on, but it was obviously dead now and he saw me bite into in, put it into my mouth and carry it away. Then, I was gone.

Very slowly and quietly Possum made his way down the back side of the tree. He sniffed around looking for evidence that would tell him what I'd been eating. What he found chilled his blood! He had found a small bone from a squirrel's hind leg. The cat, me, that he thought he had befriended, the cat he had planned on trusting, had just confirmed his worst nightmare. In Possum's mind, I may have been hunting an owl, but tonight I'd settled on a squirrel!

Who would turn up missing this time? Was it a cousin or a friend? It might even be one of Possum's own brothers or sisters. For Possum, one thing was certain. He would not trust that cat again, ever! Unfortunately, I had no idea he was even there. I had no clue that Possum was now sure I was a killer who had gone back on his word.

Possum knew he had to come up with a plan that would save the creatures in the woods from the owl he'd heard in the night. And he also had to come up with a plan to save them from me, Black Bart. It had to be foolproof. One little mistake on Possum's part at this point could mean both death and disaster.

Chapter 6

Blinded

I arrived at home very late that night. I yowled by my girl's bedroom window until she opened the front door and called for me. I went around the house, came in, and settled down on her bed for the night. I slept like a baby. There were no nightmares to disturb my sleep this time, and no intruding thoughts to claw at my conscience. Everything was going so well I felt like I could do no wrong. Yet, the truth was that I was purposefully deceiving everyone I knew, even myself. What I had been doing, what I was planning, was very wrong. Morning came early, and I was ready.

This is how I expected things to go. First, I would meet Possum by the same tree we had met at the day before. Possum would then explain his plan to get some of his bigger woodland friends to let me haul them back to the door, glare at the other cats, then let them go, much the way Tiki used to do. This would go on until the day I died, and my reputation would turn into a legend that no cat would ever be able to top. Generation upon generation of house cats would tremble at the name Black Bart. Generation upon generation of squirrels would praise that same name. I was a genius! I was a king among cats! I was Bart, Black Bart to some.

It was daytime. The cats had found the squirrel bones in the hairball that I had "coughed up". They were impressed once again. I knew the owl should have been given the credit for the hunt, but I didn't care. After all, the owl wasn't the one who brought the evidence back to the house. I imagined what I might say to the owl about my getting credit for his hunting success. "Too bad, so sad, you've been had, and I'm glad."

But I was just day dreaming. Owls were too dumb to care about the evidence of the hunt. Nevertheless, I continued to chant my new petty little poem in my head as I went into the woods. I guess that at this point, I felt like I had fooled them all and was enjoying my cunning capabilities.

I got to the tree early that morning and let out a loud "MEEE-Owww" to let Possum know I was there. I scanned the trees looking for my new friend. I was eager to hear what kind of plan he had come up with.

Not a sound was made and not a creature could be seen, except for Possum looking down at me from way out on a high limb. "Come on down!" I yelled. "I'm ready to talk."

Possum had to plan his speech carefully. He needed to bait me into helping him without putting himself in danger. He decided to attack my pride. "I'm not sure I want to talk," Possum replied. "You see, I don't know if you're able to follow through with the plan I've come up with. I'm not sure you're brave enough. And I'm not sure that you won't eat me just for suggesting it!"

"You'll never know unless you try," I shot back.

"That's exactly it! What good would it do me to come down out of the safety of the trees just to have you eat me and then go after my friends? What guarantee do I have that you won't change your mind? How can I know I can trust you?"

"I could have eaten you yesterday," I reminded Possum. "Besides, what's keeping you from sharing your plan from there? You know as well as I do that while cats can climb up trees, they are slow at getting back down, and the branches you're sitting on would never hold my weight."

"I may be able to explain my idea from here, but I can't help you carry it out without leaving the trees. I want to help you execute the plan, not me! And, like I said, I'm not sure you're brave enough."

"Me, brave enough! Try me! Wasn't it you who asked what you could do for me? Wasn't it me who spared your life? I thought we might even become friends. And now you're the one too scared to come down here and face me like a cat!" What did he mean by suggesting I wasn't brave enough? Didn't I challenge Brandy the ferocious guard dog and prevail? Didn't I fearlessly prowl the woods, even knowing there was a Great Horned Owl warning other predators to stay away?

Insults from a squirrel were too much to take. Maybe I would eat him after all. Then reality hit me like a rolled up newspaper. I could only catch him if he let me, my victory over Brandy had nothing to do with courage, and I'd actually been afraid of the owl I'd heard in the night. My old friend humiliation came back for a visit.

I had let everyone draw their own conclusions about me from what they observed. What they thought about me made sense from what they saw, but their own suspicious minds had created a web of assumptions that couldn't hold water. The other cats really didn't know me at all. I had no real friends. Most of the other cats were afraid of me. "Let them believe what they want," I told myself. I didn't care, and what they thought seemed to work in my favor. But that wasn't really who I wanted to be. Sure, I was big and strong, and proud, but I was kind and loyal, too. Or at least I thought I was.

Have you ever been rewarded when you knew very well it wasn't deserved? If so, and you were like me, you didn't say a word. I had one of the best cat reputations around. All of it was based on my getting credit for things I didn't do. Yet that wasn't enough. I wanted more, and I was willing to keep on deceiving others to get it. Maybe I did deserve the title, "the biggest, toughest, *meanest* house cat ever to prowl the woods at night." I was taking advantage of other's fears.

I didn't realize it just then, but I was a coward. I was afraid my reputation would be lost. I was afraid the other cats would make fun of me. I was afraid to do the right thing. So, without another thought, I continued to discuss with

Possum a plan for my lasting legacy. And what a plan it was!

"You're not the only predator in the woods, you know," Possum yelled from his safe perch high in the tree. "Just last night a giant bird swooped down in silence and killed my cousin Roscoe." I could hear his voice crack and could tell he was both sad and scared. I didn't know then that he really thought I was the reason for Roscoe's disappearance. "There's no way to make a deal with a creature like that. They just want to kill and eat, eat and kill."

"But I'm not like that," I returned. "If you have a good plan, I'm ready to listen. Actually, I may even get to like you." I tried to smile, but it showed my teeth and I think it had the opposite effect I was looking for. Possum scurried even higher into the tree.

From there, Possum continued with his plan, hoping he could rid the woods of other predators and scare me off at the same time. It really bothered Possum that he had misjudged me. His first impression of me was that I was kind-hearted under a rough exterior. He was usually a good judge of character, but that character had just eaten his cousin. "If you really want to be known as the greatest hunter of all time and become more famous than Tiki, you'll have to *be* the greatest. The problem isn't that you're not the biggest and the toughest, it's that the trophies that will really impress the other cats are not only tough them-selves, but they are nearly impossible to catch."

I knew at once he was talking about the Great Horned Owl. Their worst predators have headlights and wheels and are driven by people. Yeah, maybe I could take on an owl. After all, even though they have a huge wing span, they are actually only a fraction of my weight. A large one would only weigh about four pounds. But they are strong, they can fly, and their talons and beaks are wicked. They can mimic other animals and even throw their voice so it sounds like it's coming from someplace else. They can fly so quietly that you can't hear them hovering right above you. They can see even better than a cat at night, and that's when they do all their hunting. They are fiercely territorial and are likely to be the one that attacks first. This plan of Possum's was not one I liked very much. I hoped there was more to it.

Possum knew I could take on even a Great Horned Owl and win if I could get the jump on it. He also knew I would more than likely be severely wounded in the process. Infection might set in, or at the very least it would take me a while to heal, and I may not be as eager to make the woods my hunting ground the next time. There was one thing Possum knew. I couldn't be trusted! Poor Roscoe! I had once again gotten the credit for something I didn't do. Only this time I had no clue, and it wasn't working in my favor.

"You will need my help if you want to catch something like an owl, you know. It's not going to just let you know where it is, and it certainly isn't going to let you get the jump on it. You will need something for bait. You will need something to trick it into swooping down to the ground so you can pounce on it and tear it to shreds," explained Possum. "I can make the perfect decoy, but I will only do that if you keep from hunting our woods at night."

I considered his offer in silence for a few minutes. Possum's plan sounded almost too good to be true. If I could jump on the back of an owl and pin it to the ground with my sharp claws, it wouldn't have a chance to use its beak or its talons before I could make the kill.

"It's a deal. If you see me in the woods at night, I won't be hunting," I assured Possum. He wasn't so sure. I then went home looking forward to a nap on a nice warm chair before returning.

I left the house late that night in search of another owl pellet to bring back for the neighborhood cats. I made a scene out of leaving so they knew I was headed for the woods. I even started with a great "MEEE Owwww!" to make sure they heard me leave. I was determined to stay out until I found another pellet.

Silently I made my way through the winding paths among the trees. It was a much darker night, but with my cat eyes I could still see without a problem. I could hear the owl sound its regular warning, "Whoo-hoo hoooooo hoo". It wanted no competition. But that really didn't bother me, since I wasn't hunting anyway. Besides, I needed the exercise. I really did think I was too big for the owl to attack, but kept to the darkest shadows just in case.

I searched for hour upon hour to no avail. If the owl was eating, there would be pellets somewhere. Eventually I found myself near the spot where I'd found the last pellet. I sniffed and searched. I checked around nearby trees, under brush, in the grass. I searched everywhere. Finally I gave up on that spot, sharpened my claws on a tree, and started to leave. Then I saw it! It was even bigger than the last one. I wasn't sure if it even came from the same owl.

It brought back memories of my catnip ball at home. I batted at it and watched it fly, chased it down and pounced! I grabbed it with my teeth and flung it into the air just to pounce on it again. Then I heard the most terrifying scream. I looked up just in time to have my face caught by massive talons. With my mouth full, I spun to my back and kicked with my powerful hind legs. Then I ran like my life depended on it. Come to think of it, my life probably did depend on it. I now knew first hand how dangerous a Great Horned Owl could be. A large chunk of skin was missing off of my right cheek. Pain throbbed in my head and I seemed to be blind in my right eye.

Impressing the other cats was hardly on my mind when I returned home. I could only see through one eye, my face hurt, and I was seeking a warm place to sleep. I pushed through the loose boards in the fence to the back yard, spit out the slimy pellet and went straight to the front door. I yowled, and was let inside. I must have woken my girl up because she was very tired when she let me in and didn't notice my face. We both went to her bed. She crawled between her sheets, and I curled up on the top of the blankets beside her. We both fell sound asleep.

Chapter 7

A Bird's Eye View

Possum had heard my loud cry announcing to the other cats my intention to go hunt in the woods. He positioned himself in a tree near the path I used each time I came. Silently, he watched me go by, but it wasn't long before he lost me in the shadows. There was no way Possum could follow me tonight. It was simply too dark for him.

Possum's next idea was to go to the same spot where he had seen me pounce on his poor cousin Roscoe. He thought I might return to relive the glory of the moment. Once again he was right, and wrong. I did return, but it was only to look for another owl pellet. Possum traveled by jumping from tree to tree through the forest canopy. He thought he might have a good view from his cousin Roscoe's old nest, but just when he was about to jump onto the tree where Roscoe once lived, he saw something huge move in the night.

There in Roscoe's nest were not one, but two Great Horned Owls. They had taken the nest for their own. That would mean one to four young owlet hunters would be flying in the woods in as little as three months. Possum was amazed that the owls didn't hear him coming or see him with their incredible eyes. He should have been dead. How could he have been so careless?

Then he noticed why the owls hadn't seen or heard him coming. Their full attention was focused on a large black animal pouncing, batting, and snarling at some poor creature beneath them. Possum couldn't see very well in the dark. But, there I was, and in Possum's mind I'd gone back on my word again. Possum wanted to run back home, but knew he would have to stay hidden well into the next day to keep from being discovered by the owls. Then he would have to do something to end the reintroduction of predators into his woods.

Suddenly, the larger owl, the female, made a terrifying noise as she dove down to chase off the intruder. Possum watched the short struggle that followed. He couldn't see that I'd been hurt, only that I'd easily escaped the owl's attack. The scream was enough to frighten Possum into panic. Thankfully, true to his name, he froze instead of running. Running might have made him an owl snack for sure.

The small animals in the forest were now disappearing at an alarming rate with what Possum thought were three great hunters sharing the same hunting ground. Possum decided he could no longer afford to avoid me. He had to forget that he'd seen me hunting in the woods two nights in a row. He had to follow through with his plan to save his friends and relatives, no matter how dangerous it was for him. He made up his mind. He would come to the forest floor and talk to me tomorrow.

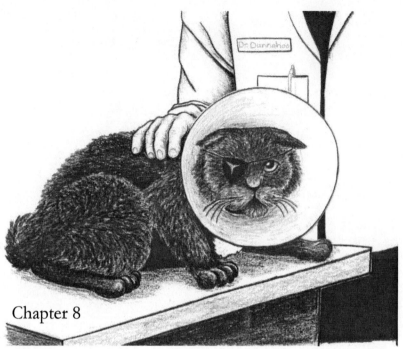

Chapter 8

Dr. Dunnahoo

My face still hurt when I woke up the next morning. This time my girl noticed it right away. It would have been pretty hard to miss. There were three claw marks deep into the muscle of my face, which was exposed where my skin had been torn away by the owl. My right eye was swollen and full of goop, and I'd left a mark on Debbie's blanket where I had rested my head.

My girl went to the bathroom and came back with some antibiotic ointment and a bandage. She carefully applied the ointment and covered only part of the wound with her bandage. It's a good thing I didn't see what she had put on my face or it would have been one more taste of humiliation. No real tom cat minds being hurt in battle, but a princess bandage to cover the wound would have been quite embarrassing.

It wasn't long before Debbie's father came into the room to take a look at my face. He decided we would have to make a trip to the veterinarian. So off we went; Debbie, her father, her mother, and her little brother David. There are three things I detest: water, mice, and car rides.

I had already destroyed several cardboard cat carriers my people tried to use to take me to the vet in the past. The carrier they now used was made of hard plastic and had metal bars on the door. It was made for dogs, so unfortunately it worked very well at keeping me in. I yowled loudly the entire trip and shredded every bit of newspaper they had put on the bottom of the carrier. Misery loves company, and my incessant yowling was bound to make others suffer for my ride.

Have you ever smelled a vet's office? It smells of bleach and fear. Only the sickest or dumbest animals are actually happy to be there. People were bound to look in my mouth, put goop in my ears, shove pills down my throat and give me a shot. Some animals who went to the vet sick never came back. Not my idea of fun!

It took two assistants to hold me down so that Dr. Dunnahoo, the veterinarian, could look at my face. One of them received the honor of a deep scratch on her arm for her trouble. My eye was infected, but thankfully, my face wasn't. They gave me a shot of penicillin. It was probably payback for scratching the nurse. Maybe she should have been the one to get the shot. They put goop in my eye and added a patch, more goop on my face, and then the worst! They put a plastic collar around my head that looked like a lamp shade to keep me from scratching my face while it healed. And I thought the princess bandage was humiliating. Just wait till the other cats saw this! The mighty Bart was about to become a freak show star.

The trip home was more miserable than the trip there. Once again, I yowled all the way. What I didn't know is that the doctor had given my people strict instructions not to let me outside, to keep petroleum jelly on my wound to keep it from scabbing over, and to make things worse, to lay off the milk and table scraps. He said I was overweight. Didn't he realize it was solid muscle? Things had gone from bad to worse.

When we finally got home, I stuck my head in the corner of the cat carrier to keep from being seen on the way to the house. I'm sure the other cats heard me. I was so miserable I had to keep yowling. When they let me out of the cage at home, I was a nervous wreck. I tried to shake the strange collar off my neck as I ran to hide under my girl's bed. All I succeeded in doing was to run into everything between the front door and the bed. I felt more like Fuzzball than Bart.

I would not be visiting the woods for a while. Possum was on his own for now.

Chapter 9

A Trap

It was over a week before my people took off the collar and let me out of the house. I kept the patch. I couldn't see out of my other eye anymore anyway, and it helped my look. While in the house I had learned to cope with only one eye. It had done horrible things to my depth perception. I was now quite uncomfortable with heights. Every time I jumped down from something I always hit the ground before I expected to, which usually resulted in my kissing the floor with my face. I also had a hard time telling distances. For example, I once tried to jump on my girl's lap at the dinner table in hopes she would slip me a piece of ham, when "WHAM!" I missed her lap, slid off the side of the chair and fell flat on my back. It would have been humiliating if I hadn't quickly jumped back to my feet and pretended nothing happened. I'm sure my people didn't notice. They were too busy laughing at something. I never did find out what was so funny.

All around the neighborhood the cats heard about my battle with the owl in the woods, so to them my patch was a badge of courage. I found I was now even able to break up cat fights with a single meow. I guess they had found rabbit bones, as well as a squirrel skull, in the pellets I'd brought back. It was a good thing for me they didn't know from where they really came.

The next day I decided it was time to venture back into the woods. I hadn't gained any weight while in the house, since my people wouldn't give me milk or food scraps. I did, however, feel a bit out of shape. I missed my walks and, to tell the truth, I missed Possum. I wondered if Possum had missed me.

It didn't take long to find him. He spotted me coming and ran down his tree to meet me.

"Are you going to eat me?" he asked right away. "Because if you are, do it quick and get it over with. I'm tired of you sneaking in here at night and killing us off. The owls are bad enough to have around without you eating us too."

"Whoa! Wait just a minute. I haven't been anywhere near the woods for over a week. I told you we had a deal. I told you I wasn't going to hunt in the woods at night." What was wrong with this squirrel? Had he finally gone off the deep end?

"Yeah, that's what you said. I wonder what kind of promises you made my cousin Roscoe before you ate him. Don't try to deny it. I saw you!" Possum's voice started to crack again. "Then you came back again the night the owl attacked you right after you killed another one of us. Who was it that time? Was it Perky, Frisky, Jumper, or one of the others that has come up missing in the last couple of weeks? I almost got eaten myself that night by an owl. Thankfully it was watching you at the same time I was. I watched you attack another one of us! I can't see that well in the dark, but I know it was you and you had attacked something!"

"No, wait! You've got it all wrong. I wasn't hunting, it was the owl. I wanted to help you. I've never killed anything." I tried to defend myself, but the damage was done.

"Liar, liar, liar, liar, liar, liar! You're a big, mean, liar!" Possum had finally lost it and flipped. He kept coming with the chatter and started poking me with his little paw. "You don't want to help us, you want to eat us. You want to blame it on the owls so you can keep coming in here and killing us. You want to drag our dead bodies back to the door so you can show off to your friends. You want us to help you bring back an owl, too, so that you can be a big shot! Liar, liar, liar, liar, liar, liar!!!"

I'd had enough from this little chatterbox. I pounced and pinned Possum to the ground. Only this time I didn't use my sharp claws. I kept them retracted in my velvety paws. I leaned down and whispered in Possum's ear, "What do a squirrel and an acorn have in common?" I paused before I answered. "They're both nuts! I didn't eat you before, and I'm not going to eat you now. I know you don't believe me, and you're probably not going to, but the truth is you need my help to get rid of that owl. I can't do it myself. If you let me, I'll prove to you I am your friend."

Possum actually started to laugh. "They're both nuts!" His laughter grew. "I love it. Do you have any more jokes?" He didn't give me time to answer. "Okay, there's no time to waste. Take that silly patch off your face and follow me."

I stared at him with my one good eye. "The patch stays! Now where are we going?"

I followed Possum deep into the woods. He climbed up to a hole in a tall tree and disappeared. He came back with his cheeks full of something. He spit them out. They were nuts, several of them still in their shells.

"Here's the plan. During the daylight when the owl is asleep, (he didn't tell me there were two of them) I'll plant these nuts on the path below the nest. You hide in the bushes, but don't move! Don't twitch a whisker or your tail! When it starts to get dark, I'll come along and start picking up the nuts. I'll die if you don't do your job. But why am I worried? You are, after all, the biggest, toughest, meanest house cat ever to prowl the woods at night." He continued, "As soon as you see the owl, pounce! If you really want to be my friend you must tackle it in the air. Otherwise, I won't be alive to be your friend. Kill it quick! Don't mess around or you'll find yourself in trouble, too. I've only survived because I've stayed in hiding every night since the owl attacked you. I'll run up the nearest tree and hide. You can then drag the owl home and be the hero you always wanted to be. That's it! That's the plan!"

I could hardly believe this squirrel was crazy enough to risk his life to save his friends. But then again, I'd seen him do it before. I was really starting to like this nutty guy. "When do we start?" I asked.

"Let's go right now! Follow me." It was the perfect time of day to sneak up to the owl and set our trap. Possum had decided this was his only chance to save his friends and relatives. He figured that by not telling me about the other owl, the battle that would come of it would rid the woods of all three of the nightmarish predators that had been wreaking havoc in his once peaceful home. He planned never to befriend a cat again, if he survived.

Both of us snuck very quietly along the ground until we found ourselves below the nest that was now occupied by the owls. While I found the perfect hiding spot in the bushes just beside the trail, Possum carefully set the nuts on the path in front of me. I dared not take a nap for fear of losing my only opportunity to help Possum. It seemed like an eternity waiting for the sun to go down. I was nervous, tired, and excited all at once. Have you ever tried to keep from fiddling with something when you were nervous? Have you ever tried to keep still when you were excited? I was doing both, but it wasn't easy!

Then it happened. It started to get dark. I waited some more. I waited even more. I started to get sleepy. My eyes were so heavy I could hardly keep them open. Then something got my attention. It was Possum scurrying down the trail, picking up nuts. I almost forgot myself and came out of my hiding place to greet him. Then I remembered.

What happened next was so sudden and so dreadful that I can still remember it. It was as if it all happened in slow motion. Without a sound the owl came from nowhere, and like a stone, hurled itself straight down on Possum.

I pounced and caught the owl right out of the air. I clamped my jaws down tight on its thick neck, killing it instantly. I could hear the bones crunch, but I couldn't hear the other owl flying in for the attack. Searing pain spread through my back as the talons took hold. It tried to lift me off the ground, but I was far too heavy for it. I shook and rolled in a flurry of blood, fur, and feathers. I tore into it with my claws and the owl returned the favor by tearing into me with its sharp powerful beak. I grabbed it with my front paws, bit its head, and started kicking as hard as I could. After kicking it several times with my powerful hind feet, I knocked it away. Only this time I didn't run. I pounced with every ounce of strength I had left in me. I made the kill.

I collapsed with exhaustion and fell asleep. I woke up early the next morning and hurt all over my body. My fur was sticky with blood. I was incredibly sore, but everything seemed to work alright. I figured Possum had gone home, expecting me to be dead. I got up slowly and stretched. It felt like I'd been run over by a motorcycle and gotten caught in the chain.

Then I noticed something strange. There, lying on the ground, were two Great Horned Owls and one large gray squirrel. It was Possum. With my one eye I must not have hit the first owl when I planned. The owl was able to grasp onto Possum with one foot before I could kill it.

Possum was badly hurt and still unconscious. So there I was. I had a choice to make. I could bring back not one, but two Great Horned Owls to the front porch. I could limp by the other cats showing them my wounds and taunting them with the now true fact that a one-eyed cat, Black Bart, was indeed the greatest hunter of all time.

Or, I could do the right thing. I could bring Possum back to the house, give him to my girl, and hope she could save him. It really wasn't a choice at all.

As I carefully picked Possum up by the back of his neck, I finally found what I had been looking for. Peace. If Possum recovered, I would tell him everything from the beginning. I wanted Possum to forgive me. I no longer cared what the other cats thought. Let them laugh. It wouldn't change a thing.

Chapter 10

Home

I could hear the other squirrels start to chatter loudly as I gently carried Possum through the darkness of the night back to the girl who had so kindly bottle fed me as a kitten. I bore the pain of the horrid battle to give Possum the most comfortable journey I could. Well, as comfortable as you could make someone you were carrying by the neck with your teeth. I moved slowly, in order not to stumble over branches or roots protruding from the ground.

Possum's friends and relatives watched from the trees. The owls were dead and would no longer pose a threat. I, however, had survived. They were puzzled by my choice of trophies. Why was it that I had chosen Possum to take back when I could have brought back two Great Horned Owls? They couldn't tell that Possum was still breathing and were sad to see him being dragged off by the great cat, but they were proud at the same time. His sacrifice had not gone unnoticed. The other squirrels had felt for a long time that Possum was crazy. They had advised him to do what squirrels had done for generations. Be quick, stay hidden, and avoid cats at all costs.

When I arrived at the back fence, I found the boards no longer loose. With Possum in my mouth, I would have to go through the alley, around the other houses and along the street in front of everyone. The fence was too tall to just jump, especially with Possum in my mouth.

I walked down the street slowly. My thoughts were on Possum and whether or not he would survive the night. There were cats looking for mice, and others sitting on their front porches washing their faces with their paws. Some were waiting by their doors to come in for the night. All of them stopped what they were doing to watch me bring in this squirrel. I couldn't guess what was going through their minds, but as I said before, I really didn't care this time. My friend was badly hurt and needed help.

As I reached the front porch, I carefully set Possum down and started yowling at the front door. The other cats could see that I was obviously wounded and were looking forward to me entering the house. Then they would gather around to see the squirrel that had given me such a beating. However, they would certainly be disappointed. When Debbie came to the door to let me in, I brought my trophy with me. All the other cats would find was a little blood. Some of the blood belonged to me, and the rest belonged to Possum.

The first thing I did when entering the house was to set Possum down in front of Debbie. Her face looked sad and I could tell she was about to scold me for being a "Bad Cat". Fortunately, Possum had awakened and had enough strength left in him to get up. He started dragging his back end toward the couch. I could tell he was scared and was looking for a place to hide.

Debbie tried to pick him up. He managed to bite her hard enough to draw blood. She yelped, quickly let go, and went to get her parents. Possum pulled himself under the couch, collapsed with exhaustion, and started to shake. I went to comfort him, to tell him everything was going to be alright. I was intercepted. Debbie's little brother heard the excitement and came running to see what was happening. He saw me, tired, hurt, and bleeding. He carefully picked me up and started looking at the large puncture wounds on my back.

"Dad!" he yelled, "Bart's been in another fight. We're going to have to take him back to the vet."

Debbie and her parents came into the room. Her parents came straight over to me, but Debbie was more worried about Possum and went over to look for him under the couch. That was okay with me. I was tough and had been hurt before. I would be just fine. Possum was another story.

"Dad, he's still here," she said, carefully keeping her distance. She didn't want to get bitten again.

"Let me see," said her father. "That squirrel is never going to make it. Go get a towel so I can catch it. I'll put it outside for the other cats."

"Nooooooo!" I heard Debbie cry. "You can't! It's not his fault Bart attacked him!"

"Cool! Can I catch it, Dad?" David said. "Way to go Bart!"

Great, just what I needed. David had no idea what had happened and was proud of me. He handed me to his mom and raced down the hall to get a towel. Debbie was crying.

As they were trying to catch Possum, Debbie's mom exclaimed, "David is right, dear. Bart needs to go back to the vet."

"Can we take the squirrel too?" Debbie stopped crying and looked with hope at her mom, "Pleeeeese! I'll take good care of it."

"No way!" her mom answered. "It bit you, and just look at what it did to Bart! It might be rabid. When was your last tetanus shot?"

By this time David had Possum safely wrapped up in a towel. Possum's big frightened eyes must have gotten David's attention because he didn't take Possum to the door. Instead, he turned to his dad with puppy dog eyes and said, "Yeah. Please, Dad, can we take the squirrel to the vet too? Shouldn't we find out if it really does have rabies?"

"David does have a point, dear," said Debbie's father as he took Possum from David. "They might want to check the squirrel. If it is rabid, there might be more infected animals in the area. As much as I hate to say it, I think we're going to have to take them both."

Debbie ran over and gave her brother a big hug. It was one of the few times I saw her actually be nice to her younger brother. Most of the time, they just fought with each other. Everything was looking up. We were both going to the vet. Whether or not we would both come back was another story.

"Go get the carrier for Bart," Debbie's dad told her. Debbie rushed off to get it.

"Can I hold him Dad? He's hurt pretty bad, and if I hold him he might not yowl so much," David asked.

The last trip to the vet was fresh on his mind as he answered. "Let's take the carrier just in case we need it. You'll have to hold on to him tightly. I don't want a wounded cat bleeding all over our car. I'll hold the squirrel. Dear, you'll have to drive." Then out the door we went.

I have to admit. I was really starting to like David. He'd never paid much attention to me before, but he sure made my trip to the vet more pleasant. Possum slept most of the way there. Possum and I were both a wreck and badly in need of medical attention.

We were carried into the veterinarian's office. Debbie's father and David sat down on some chairs by the receptionist while Debbie and her mother went to the front desk.

"I'm surprised to see you back so soon," said the receptionist at the desk. "How is Bart doing?"

"Not too well. I'm afraid he's been in another fight. He brought this squirrel in the house and both of them look awful," said Debbie's mother. "We were just going to bring Bart in, but my husband thought that Dr. Dunnahoo might want to check the squirrel for rabies. It's hard to believe that a squirrel could do so much damage to a cat Bart's size."

"We'll have the doctor take a look," said the receptionist.

Chapter 11

Good News

"Well hello there, Bart. I hear you brought a friend with you today," Dr. Dunnahoo declared as he walked into the waiting area. "Please bring him back so I can take a look at him. You can bring the squirrel, too. Please go right into Room 3 and I'll be with you in a moment."

The assistant took me from David's arms, set me down on the examining table, and started cleaning the wounds on my back. "Easy now, Bart, I'm not going to hurt you." I could still see the scar from the scratch I made on her arm. I could see she was happy I didn't struggle this time. "Wow! One thing is for sure, that squirrel didn't cause these wounds! Wait till the vet sees this. Bart, you are one tough cat. Would you please hold him here? I think I'd better get the doctor."

The doctor came into the room. "Hey, big fella, let's take a look at those wounds. The nurse says they're pretty deep." Dr. Dunnahoo started examining me. It seemed that everywhere on my body he was able to find a puncture, scratch, or wound. The tips of my ears were even missing.

"This cat looks like he's been through World War III," he announced. "These wounds sure didn't come from a squirrel. Fortunately, there doesn't appear to be any broken bones or internal bleeding. The six wounds on his back are particularly deep, but I don't see any major damage. He will need several stitches. Then I'll give him a shot of antibiotics. He won't need any special care this time, except to keep him inside and warm. I want you to check his wounds for infection daily and call me if things start looking worse. Oh, and you may want to get him some cat treats. I know I told you to lay off the milk and table scraps, but after what he's been through, he deserves a little pampering." I was given several shots, but they didn't hurt much compared to the pain I was already in. Then the doctor stitched up the wounds on my back.

"Now let me take a look at that squirrel." Dr. Dunnahoo took me off the table and handed me to David. Then he took Possum from Debbie's father and carefully unwrapped the towel. "Hi, little guy. I hope you're in better shape than your friend here." There were similar marks on Possum's back. He only had three of them, though, and they weren't nearly as deep. It was a good thing, too, because Possum was quite small compared to me. "What you have here is a very frightened little squirrel," said Dr. Dunnahoo. "He's actually in pretty good shape. Whatever attacked Bart also attacked this little guy. My guess is maybe an owl. The muscles just above his hind legs have been torn into some, but he'll actually be just fine. It's too bad animals can't talk. I bet these two would tell one crazy story. I'm sure it doesn't have rabies, but as a wild animal it'll have to be turned back loose."

"Please, Dad," said David, "you heard what he said. The squirrel will be okay. Can we take him home?"

"I don't know. What do you think, doctor?" Debbie's father asked.

"I don't see why you couldn't take care of it in that cage you haul Bart around in, but I wouldn't let it loose or get your fingers too close. They can really bite! You'll have to make sure it has food and water, and when it gets to where it can run around the cage, you'll have to let it loose."

"Yes!" David yelled with a huge grin on his face. I agreed with him completely. I couldn't wait to get back home where I could tell Possum everything.

The trip home was uneventful, and since they put Possum in the cage, I got to ride on a lap. I rode on Debbie's this time. I guess she must have forgiven me after she found out I didn't attack Possum after all. David was so excited about taking Possum home, I wasn't sure he would be able to let him go back to the woods. I latched on to Debbie's little finger, started purring, and slept through the rest of the trip.

I woke up when we pulled into the driveway. I knew they would keep me in the house for a while, and I was glad. I was in no hurry to start another adventure, at least not yet.

What I did want to do was to give Possum a long overdue apology and ask for his forgiveness. I had let him, and even led him, to believe so many things about myself that just weren't true. I wanted him to forgive me, of course, but I would certainly understand if he didn't. I wanted to tell him I would be his friend if he would give me the chance. I wanted him to know that I really was a cat of my word.

David set up Possum's cage in the second bathroom. His father had left for work and his mother wanted him to clean his room. So he gave Possum some water and peanuts and left the door open while he started picking up the mess in his room.

No one was paying any attention to me, and although I really wanted a nap, I thought I'd better talk to Possum first. He was hiding in the back corner of the cage when I got there. "Hi," I said.

"Go away!" he replied.

This was going to be harder than I thought. "What's wrong? The doctor said you are going to recover and they have to let you go when you do."

"Like that's really going to help!" muttered Possum. "The doctor said you were going to be fine too. That means you will be back to hunt in our woods. I failed. I wanted to make it safe."

"Oh come on. Do you still believe I've been hunting in the woods? Well, I guess that would be my fault too," I continued. "It's time for the truth. Actually, the truth is way overdue.

I was asked by the other cats to bring back some evidence of my hunts. They thought I was a great hunter, but they wanted proof to be sure. When the owls came and I couldn't find you in the woods, I stumbled upon an owl pellet. The owl had eaten your cousin at least eight hours before he had coughed up the pellet. That's what you saw me carry back. It was just a pellet. It worked so well at fooling the other cats that I came back the next night for another one. I played with it for a while, and then I was attacked. So you see, I never did kill anything. It was those two owls that attacked me. I wanted to be your friend. I still do. Will you forgive me? I never was going to start hunting you guys. I knew I couldn't do that the night I met you. Besides, I'm really a lousy hunter. Only now I don't care what the other cats think. From now on I'm just going to be myself."

"So you really didn't bring me home to eat me alive in front of the other cats?" asked Possum. "Is that why you brought me in the house?"

"Of course I didn't want to eat you. Don't you think two dead owls would have been more impressive than one live squirrel?" I was surprised Possum didn't catch on to that immediately. Yet, he had convinced himself so completely that I was the enemy, I guess he wasn't thinking straight. Panic will do that to a squirrel.

"Yes, I forgive you," said Possum. "But only on one condition."

"Anything," I said, "just tell me what it is."

"Well, you see, I really misjudged you, Bart. At first I thought maybe you were nice. I thought maybe you would be our friend like Tiki was and help us. Once I found the squirrel bone from the owl pellet, and thought I'd just watched you eat one of us, I decided you were a backstabbing killer. I wasn't about to trust you, or be your friend. In fact, I knew there were two owls. I counted on it. I figured that even if I died, the second owl would hurt you so badly that I would have gotten rid of all three of you and made the woods safe. You got hurt because I wanted you gone. I'm sorry, Bart. If it's not too late, can we still be friends?"

"Tell me Possum, how is a cat like a good friendship?" I asked.

"I don't know, how?" Possum replied.

"When in trouble and going down, they make things right and land on their feet."

Chapter 12

Conclusion

So now you know how I got to look the way I do. I've since made friends with many of the cats in the neighborhood. I even told them about the owls and took them into the woods to see the remains of the two owls I had fought. All that's left now is just a pile of feathers and dry bones. I made a vow to help keep predators away from the woods as long as I was alive. That promise led me to many more adventures.

I also told the other cats that they had better stick to mice and leave the squirrels alone. You see, I was Bart, Black Bart to some. I was the biggest, toughest, ugliest house cat ever to prowl the woods at night. I was Bart, friend to Possum. I was Bart, defender of the woodland creatures. Not only did I apologize for my deceptions, but I changed my behavior. You see, character is developed by life's experiences, choices have consequences, honesty is the best policy, and friendship is better than fame. I am, in humble respect…

Yours Truly,

BLACK BART

- From the Author -

Dear Reader,

The end of a good story always brings a bittersweet moment. You can't wait to find out how the story ends. But then, when the end comes, you wish there was more. Well this time, there is.

I have included the first chapter of <u>The Adventures of Black Bart: An Encounter with Regret</u>. Please read on, and try to guess what lesson Bart will learn in his next adventure.

Yours Truly,
David C. Atchison

The Adventures of Black Bart:

An Encounter with Regret

By: David C. Atchison

Chapter 1: *The Interloper*

I woke up from my nightly slumber to the sound of tiny claws scratching frantically on a glass pane. My girl, Debbie, was still sleeping soundly as I stood up slowly. I wasn't quite asleep, yet not completely awake either. I stretched my back and looked around the room, expecting to see a mangy little mouse trapped inside the glass cabinet that housed my girl's collection of treasured items. I hate mice!

What I actually saw was a squirrel, my best friend Possum, madly trying to get my attention from outside one of the bedroom windows. It was a relief to see Possum rather than the mouse I expected, but I was quite surprised that he had braved the dangers of our neighborhood and come to my house without my protection.

You see, I'm just one of a hundred cats that live in my neighborhood nestled between the big city and the forty-acre wood where Possum lives. Many of the other hunters would consider a squirrel like Possum a trophy worth leaving on a doorstep. This is a common way cats show off their hunting abilities. Yes, around here, a squirrel on a doorstop would be a claim to the coveted reputation of a great hunter. Even more, it would be a direct challenge to my rule as top cat in the neighborhood.

I am Bart. Some call me Black Bart. Black as midnight with one small patch of white on my chest, I'm the biggest, toughest, ugliest house cat ever to prowl the streets at night. I am Bart, friend to Possum, protector of the woodland creatures, and thirty pounds of solid muscle no cat would ever dare to challenge in combat. I had established a well known law in our neighborhood; if a cat is to hunt, it must stick to mice and birds.

You see, Possum more than once risked his life to save his friends, and I myself saved Possum's life after learning the importance of true friendship.

Character is developed by life's experiences, and I'd come to realize that you never finish developing character. The day I first met Regret was one of those experiences.

I sprang off the bed to land on the window sill. Unfortunately, I misjudged the distance and slammed into the glass like an unsuspecting bird trying to fly through a closed window. Worse than the pain I now felt was the humiliation, as I struggled to regain my balance. Rather than fall, I pushed off the wooden ledge with my front feet and landed safely in a basket full of dirty laundry. This was not an action becoming the great Black Bart. Unfortunately, it was all too common.

I lost the sight in my right eye during a mighty struggle with a great horned owl and have worn a patch to cover that unsightly part of my face ever since. Having one eye does horrible things to a cat's depth perception, and makes judging distance during a jump rather difficult.

My concern for Possum outweighed my humiliation and gave me the strength to try again. I was now wide awake and had to find out what that crazy squirrel was up to now.

"What is it?" I asked.

Possum stopped scratching and started chattering. I couldn't hear a thing he was saying through the closed window, but could tell that Possum was very worried about something. I put my paw up against the glass to signal him that I'd be right down, and jumped down from the window sill. I was glad to see that my girl was sound asleep and didn't see me hitting the window. Possum was now on a tree branch, looking down toward the front door.

I yowled loudly to wake my girl and trotted down the stairs to start yowling at the back door. Thankfully, I didn't have to wait for Debbie to make it downstairs. Her father was already awake and more than happy to let me outside so my incessant yowling would cease.

Possum knew I disliked heights, and that there was no way I would risk climbing up the tree outside Debbie's window, so he scurried down the tree trunk to meet me.

"Help! You must help! It's a cat! A big cat! An ugly cat! A hungry cat!" Possum squeaked out the words so quickly that I almost couldn't understand him.

"Where?" I inquired.

"He was in the woods hunting. I think he's a stray," Possum answered.

I pondered this. A stray in our neighborhood was an unusual site; an unwelcome vagabond that was certain to be up to no good. I'd never met a stray cat before, but I'd heard the stories. You can recognize them by their unkempt matted hair, their bony frame, and the wild hunger in their eyes.

"Do you know where he is now?" I asked.

"No," Possum answered, "but I sure would like you to walk me back home. He'll be no match for you if we happen to run into him.

"Let's go." There was no way I would let Possum go back to the woods alone. With all the chattering Possum had done, I was sure the unsavory newcomer would be hiding in the shadows to catch Possum upon his return home.

The hole in the backyard fence that was once my favorite gateway to the alley between the house and the woods had been repaired. Possum would have no trouble scurrying his way up the fence, but heights were something I preferred to avoid. If the other cats saw me fall off the six-foot fence, it would surely damage my reputation. I wasn't too sure I could even jump to the top without having some kind of mishap. Just imagine if my first encounter with this diabolical stray included my falling off a fence! The stray might even catch and kill Possum before I could recover!

The only other option was to take Possum to the front of the house and go around the block to the alley. This would take us onto the sidewalk along the main street in front of several houses and neighboring cats. I really wanted to talk to them to see what they might know about the interloper that had trespassed into our neighborhood, but first things first. Right now I had to concentrate on getting Possum back home safely.

We passed several cats along the way. All of them watched with envy and contempt as the great cat, me, escorted Possum down the street. In their eyes, I was a king among cats and a mighty hunter with no equal. What bothered them so much was that I protected what they saw as food. While my trophies included some of the more deadly predators they had ever heard about, I would not allow them to hunt in the woods. To them, it was just plain disgraceful that I had befriended a squirrel!

I saw Chester, a light orange tabby with a large patch of white on his chest, licking his paws and cleaning his face on his front door step. There was Muffy, another black cat like me and a terrific bird hunter, perched beneath a bird feeder. We passed Thomas, Fluffy, Sunny, and Lucky, among others. All of them stopped what they were doing and watched us slowly pass by.

I kept my eyes peeled for the stranger who posed such a threat to my friend; for the dirty scoundrel who dared hunt in the woods I so diligently protected.

Just to think of this stray made my blood boil. What gave him the right to come to our neighborhood uninvited, to steal our cat food, chase and fight with our friends, dig through our garbage and yowl on our fences? I couldn't wait to meet this undeserving, unsavory dredge of society. I would teach him never to invade my happy home.

As we reached the corner, the last house on the block and the home of the cat- killing guard dog named Brandy, I made it a point to walk extra close to the fence. I wanted to stay between the fenced yard that housed one of the most ferocious dogs known to catkind, and my best friend Possum. I also wanted to have a little fun at Brandy's expense.

I once had the fortunate experience of meeting Brandy face to face. Well, I guess it wasn't really face to face. It was more like his snarling mouthful of razor sharp teeth to my tail as I ran for my life. I said fortunate because I escaped and Brandy ended up stuck by his own collar on a jagged board in a hole in the back of his own dog house. To this day, it remains the most celebrated event among cats in our neighborhood. Cats from all over heard the commotion and clamored to the top of Brandy's fence to get a belly-busting laugh at Brandy whimpering with nothing but his back side sticking out his doghouse door, while I sat on the peak of his doghouse and delighted in the sweet sound of admiration.

If Brandy's hatred for cats could have gotten any worse, it would have that day. Brandy was short on brains, but long on memory. He thought I tricked him and trapped him by his collar on purpose, and he never forgot it. The only thing that matched Brandy's hatred of me was his fear that I would humiliate him once again.

I listened intently, knowing Brandy's curiosity would get the best of him. He was always sniffing at the fence for some smaller animal to scare witless. He knew I sometimes passed his fence, but he couldn't help himself. This time I was ready. When I heard him sniff right beside me on the other side of the fence, and knew that he knew it was me by the scent, I spit, hissed, and swatted at the crack between the boards. And, like always, Brandy whimpered and ran back to his dog house, being careful not to stick his head through the hole in the back.

Possum and I continued around the next corner and into the alley. This was where I really needed to keep my good eye open. The stray could be anywhere. Possum stayed on my left side where I could see him easily. We wouldn't stop unless we met the stray beast or until I watched Possum scurry safely up his tree in the woods.

The summer day was a scorcher, with the sun shining on my black fur. Normally it had the makings of a good cat nap, but now I had to stay alert. When we stepped onto the path into the cool shade of the woods, I took a deep breath of the forest air and was refreshed. I loved these woods! They were full of fond memories and exciting adventures.

I still hadn't spotted the stray when Possum scampered up his tree, but promised I'd keep a lookout and check up on him later to make sure everything was okay. I thought about checking the woods, but decided to question my neighbors first…

To read the rest of this book ask for:

The Adventures of Black Bart:
An Encounter with Regret
By: David C. Atchison

at your local book store or visit us online at:

www.BlackBartAdventures.com